# William Shakespeare

# A Midsummer Night's Dream

### Retold by
## Marcia Williams

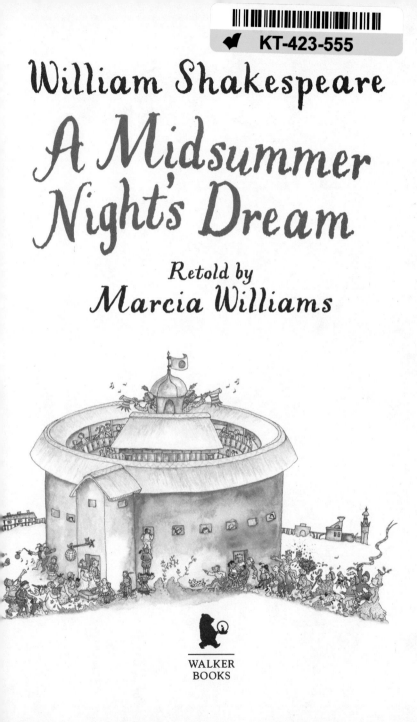

WALKER
BOOKS

# William Shakespeare

# A Midsummer Night's Dream

First published 2015 by Walker Books Ltd
87 Vauxhall Walk, London SE11 5HJ

2 4 6 8 10 9 7 5 3 1

This book has been typeset in Kennerly Regular

Printed and bound in Germany

British Library Cataloguing in Publication Data:
a catalogue record for this book is available from the British Library

ISBN 978-1-4063-6272-5

www.walker.co.uk

For Flora

# Contents

## In which Hermia and Lysander flee from Athens.

The laws in ancient Athens were extremely harsh. One of the more outrageous laws decreed that a daughter must marry the man of her father's choice. If she chose to disobey her father, she risked having to live out her days in a nunnery – or, worse, forfeit her life. You would think that fathers would let their daughters choose their own husbands, but some of them would not. Take the grand

Athenian gentleman Egeus, for example.
He was a tyrant, and he had ordered his
pretty, dark-eyed daughter Hermia to marry
a young noble called Demetrius. Demetrius
was young, good-looking and rich, and he
loved Hermia – but Hermia did not love him.
She loved his friend, Lysander, and Lysander
loved her. The trouble was that Hermia's
best friend, Helena, who was as tall and
ungainly as Hermia was small and dainty,
adored Demetrius with an all-consuming
passion.

As a result of all this, not one of them was
happy.

Hermia was as stubborn as her father
and would not agree to marry Demetrius, so
Egeus brought her to the court of Theseus,

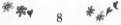

Duke of Athens. Surely the duke could persuade her to change her mind?

"Full of vexation come I, with complaint against my child," grumbled Egeus.

"What say you, Hermia?" said the duke. "Be advised, fair maid, your father should be as a god!"

"I would my father look'd but with my eyes!" said Hermia.

Theseus was about to get married himself, so he was inclined to be sympathetic

towards Hermia. He gave her four days to choose between love and duty. "Take time to pause," he gently advised her.

But love never pauses – it rushes on, untamed. Being in love himself, the duke should perhaps have realized this! Besides, those as headstrong and fiery as Hermia do not listen to advice, even from the Duke of Athens.

"O hell! To choose love by another's eyes!"

Hermia grumbled to Lysander when they were alone. Unable to bear the thought of parting, Lysander and Hermia agreed to flee Athens and marry where Athenian law could not touch them. They confided their plan to no one except Helena.

Hermia hoped the news that she was leaving and was

about to marry Lysander would cheer Helena up – it would give her a chance to woo Demetrius! Poor Helena; she could not understand why Demetrius chose Hermia's scorn over her love.

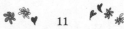

"Take comfort: he no more shall see my face," Hermia told her friend. "Lysander and myself will fly this place. Farewell, sweet playfellow: pray thou for us. And good luck grant thee thy Demetrius!" She smiled and hugged her friend goodbye.

That night, while their family and friends slept, Hermia and Lysander fled to the woods, away from the city and its cruel law. Unfortunately Helena, hoping to gain

Demetrius's attention, told him of Hermia and Lysander's flight. But her plan did not work. Demetrius was obsessed with Hermia and determined to get her back, so he set out after the runaway lovers. All the lovelorn Helena could do was to follow Demetrius, declaring her love every second of the way!

Once they reached the woods, Demetrius turned on Helena. "I love thee not, therefore pursue me not!" he cried, angrily.

Still she dogged his footsteps, so again he turned on her. "I tell you I do not nor I cannot love you!"

"And even for that do I love you the more," sniffed Helena. "I am your spaniel."

Try as he might, Demetrius could not shake her off. So the pair continued deeper and deeper into the woods, searching along every path for Lysander and Hermia.

In which we meet the
players and the fairies.

Demetrius and Helena were so involved
with their search that they didn't notice
they were not the only ones in the wood
that night.

In one glade, six Athenian workmen
were secretly rehearsing a play for Duke
Theseus's
wedding to
Hippolyta.

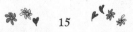

If their play was chosen they would be richly rewarded, so they took the rehearsal seriously and were eager to entertain.

Most eager of all was Bottom the weaver, who thought he should play every part! "Let me play Thisby," he lisped. "I'll speak in a monstrous little voice. Let me play the lion too," he roared. "I will roar, that I will do any man's heart good to hear me!"

However, Peter Quince, who was directing the play, would only allow Bottom to play the lover, Pyramus. He made sure everyone got a part – he even had actors playing moonshine and a wall!

In another glade hid stranger folk than these. For the wood was the fairy kingdom of King Oberon and Queen Titania and

their fairies, sprites, goblins and elves.
The king and queen had recently quarrelled
over a changeling boy that Queen Titania had
stolen. King Oberon wanted to have
the boy for himself, but Titania would not let
him go. So when Oberon came across
his queen and her fairies that night he was
not pleased.

"Ill met by moonlight, proud Titania,"
he grumbled darkly.

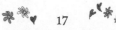

"What! Jealous Oberon!" returned Titania. "Fairies, skip hence: I have forsworn his bed and company."

Oberon decided to play a trick on Titania. He sent his naughty sprite, Puck, to find a plant called Love-in-idleness. If you put its juice on someone's eyes as they slept, they would love the first creature they saw upon waking.

Puck's eyes glinted with delight. There was nothing he loved more than tricks and trouble! "I'll put a girdle round about the earth in forty minutes!" he cried as he vanished into the night.

## In which Puck makes a crucial error.

Now, as it happened, Demetrius and Helena passed close to where Oberon sat waiting for Puck's return. Oberon could not help

overhearing what passed between the pair.

"I am sick when I do look on thee,"
Demetrius shouted at Helena.

"And I am sick when I look not on you,"
she sniffed.

Then off they went again, Demetrius
chasing Hermia, and Helena chasing
Demetrius!

Oberon was touched by Helena's
devotion, which was so unlike his own
queen's, and he decided that she should have
Demetrius. So, when Puck returned, Oberon
told him to wait until the couple slept and
then anoint Demetrius's eyelids with the
juice of the magic plant. Demetrius would
then wake to see Helena, and love her for
ever more.

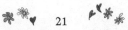

21

"Thou shalt know the man by the Athenian garments he hath on," Oberon said.

"Fear not, my lord, your servant shall do so," cried Puck, vanishing in an instant.

Meanwhile, Oberon had his own plan. He set out in search of his sleeping queen. When he found her, he squeezed the flower's magic juice upon her eyelids.

"What thou seest, when thou dost wake, do it for thy true-love take, be it ounce,

or cat, or bear. Wake when some vile thing is near," he whispered in Titania's ear. Then he vanished into the shadows to wait and watch.

Puck was also busy anointing a pair of eyes with the flower's juice. "Weeds of Athens he doth wear: this is he, my master said," he mused. Only unfortunately it was the wrong "he"! Puck had mistaken Lysander for Demetrius and had put the flower's juice on his eyes as he lay

close to Hermia. And then, as luck would
have it, Helena, still in pursuit of Demetrius,
tripped over Lysander in the dark and woke
him. So Lysander instantly forgot his love
for Hermia and fell in love with Helena!

"Not Hermia, but Helena I love," he cried.

"Do not say so," exclaimed Helena.

"Wherefore was I to this keen mockery born?"

Shocked and confused by Lysander's unexpected declaration of love, Helena ran off. Lysander followed close on her heels, crying, "To honour Helen, and to be her knight!"

Thus poor Hermia woke alone.

 25

"Lysander! Alack, where are you? I swoon almost with fear," she cried. Terrified, she set out in search of her beloved Lysander.

## In which both passions and tempers flare.

All this while Titania slept on, unaware that the troupe of Athenians, led by Bottom and Peter Quince, had chosen to rehearse their play in a nearby glade.

"Speak, Pyramus – Thisby, stand forth," Peter Quince ordered his actors.

It was the perfect opportunity for Puck to play one of his tricks, for Titania's eyelids still glistened with magic juice and

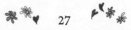

he wanted to make sure she fell in love
with something truly vile when she awoke.
So he cast a spell on Bottom the weaver.
Suddenly, in the middle of the play, Bottom
came out from behind a bush with his head
turned into a hairy ass's head!

"O monstrous!" shouted Peter Quince. "O
strange! We are haunted. Pray masters, fly!"

The other actors fled in fright. Puck
guided Bottom by magic to the sleeping

28

Titania's side. There he left him, and retired
to watch events unfold.

Poor Bottom didn't realize he had been
transformed. He thought his friends were
making fun of him. "I see their knavery,"
he said. "This is to make an ass of me, to
fright me if they could. I will sing, that
they shall hear I am not afraid." But he
was quaking with fear! Bottom sang with
an ass's bray:

"*The ousel-cock, so black of hue,*

*With orange-tawny bill,*

*The throstle with his note so true,*

*The wren with little quill.*"

"What angel wakes me from my flowery bed?" cried Titania, woken by the sound. When she saw Bottom, she instantly fell in love with him, even though he had an ass's head!

Bottom was not displeased by the queen's attention, especially when she ordered her fairies to attend his every whim.

"Pease-blossom! Cobweb! Moth! And Mustardseed! Be kind and courteous to this gentleman; hop in his walks, and gambol in his eyes; feed him with apricots and dewberries," she cried.

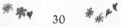

Puck reported all this to the delighted Oberon. As they were talking, Demetrius and Hermia paused close by.

"Stand close," whispered Oberon, "this is the same Athenian."

"This is the woman," replied Puck, "but not this the man!"

Oberon realized that Puck had made a mistake: Demetrius still loved Hermia, who

still loved Lysander — but now, Lysander
loved Helena, who still loved Demetrius!

Demetrius was overcome with exhaustion
and lay down to rest, while Hermia plunged
into the nearest thicket in search of
Lysander.

"What hast thou done?" cried Oberon,
annoyed by his sprite's mistake. He sent
Puck to fetch Helena.

"I go, I go; look how I go," cried Puck.

Meanwhile Oberon anointed Demetrius's weary eyelids with the flower's juice. "When his love he doth espy, let her shine as gloriously as the Venus of the sky," he whispered.

At that moment, Puck returned, drawing Helena along behind him with an invisible thread. Lysander followed her, still bewitched and love-sick!

Demetrius awoke, and when his eyes rested on Helena it was as if he was seeing her for the first time. The arrow of love pierced his heart and he threw himself at her feet. "O Helena, goddess, nymph, perfect, divine!"

Helena, far from being happy, believed

Demetrius was mocking her. "O spite! O hell!" she cried. "I see you all are bent to set against me for your merriment."

When Hermia arrived on this scene, she quickly understood that both Lysander and Demetrius now loved Helena. Hermia was beside herself with anger, and screamed abuse at her friend. "O me! You juggler! You canker-blossom! You thief of love!"

"You puppet, you!" retaliated Helena.

"Thou painted maypole!" shrieked
Hermia, flying at Helena, her nails like a
cat's claws.

Lysander and Demetrius looked on, and
when they could bear it no more they went
to find space for their own duel.

Left to themselves, Hermia and Helena
couldn't wait to get away from each other.

"I will not trust you, nor longer stay in
your curst company," declared Helena, using
her long legs to vanish into the wood.

"This is thy negligence," Oberon declared to Puck as he came out of the shadows.

"Believe me, King of Shadows, I mistook," protested Puck – although he was enjoying every minute of the drama! However, Oberon wanted the harm that the magic had done to be undone with another magic flower. So on Oberon's orders, Puck drew the lovers into the wood.

"Up and down, up and down," he sang, "I will lead them up and down." Puck led them this way and that way, through bush and briar. They could hear each other, but they could not see each other. At last, thoroughly confused and exhausted, they fell asleep – all within the same glade. Puck was delighted with his work!

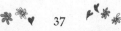

As Puck squeezed the flower's juice on
Lysander's eyes, he sang:

"*When thou wak'st,*

*Thou taks't*

*True delight*

*In the sight*

*Of thy former lady's eye!*

*Jack shall have Jill; nought shall go ill.*"

With these words, Puck left the sleeping
lovers and vanished to watch what would
happen when they awoke.

For once, Puck had not caused more mischief. Hermia woke to Lysander's love and Helena to Demetrius's. All anger was forgotten as these young Athenians were reunited in both friendship and love.

Meanwhile, in another part of the wood, Bottom lay sleeping in Titania's loving arms. Oberon looked down at them with amusement and then put an antidote on

Titania's eyelids. "See as thou was wont to see," he whispered.

Then he woke Titania. She was mortified that Oberon had found her with a snoring ass in her arms! "My Oberon, what visions have I seen! Methought I was enamour'd of an ass," she cried. To cover her confusion

she promised to give the changeling boy to Oberon. Oberon was satisfied at last! He called for music and danced happily

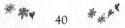

away with Titania, leaving Puck to turn
Bottom back to his usual self.

In which many
couples are wed.

The day was nearly dawning and Duke
Theseus was leading his hounds on an early
morning hunt with his love, Hippolyta, and

Hermia's father, Egeus. When they came across the runaway lovers, Egeus was still eager to force Hermia to marry Demetrius! "I beg the law!" he demanded of Duke Theseus.

Luckily for Hermia, this was Duke Theseus's wedding day. When he saw the young people so in love and paired off so happily, he overruled Egeus. He bade the whole party return with him to Athens and resolved that all three couples would wed that very day: he and Hippolyta, Hermia

and Lysander, and Helena and Demetrius.
Everyone was delighted, except Egeus, who
grumbled all the way home!

After the wedding ceremonies, the motley
troupe of actors − including Bottom, who
had his old head back − were called to put
on their play. They put their all into every
part! "Roar!" went the lion and "shine" went

the moon, so that the audience cried, "Well roared, Lion" and "Well shone, Moon." The play earned them much money and applause!

As the players departed, the duke called for music and everyone celebrated the end of an eventful day with a dance. Even Egeus smiled – he seemed quite pleased that his daughter was neither dead nor banished,

but dancing in the arms of Lysander, the man she truly loved.

"The iron tongue of midnight hath told twelve," yawned the duke, as the music faded. "Lovers to bed; 'tis almost fairy time."

And so the whole company, at last restored to happy harmony, retired to bed.

For a moment the hall was left in quiet darkness. Then came the fairy king and queen, attended by Puck and a whole train of fairies, elves and goblins, and they banished the darkness with fairy light. They had come to bless the palace of Duke Theseus and all who slept there – a perfect end to the story, or maybe to a midsummer night's dream in an enchanted wood...

**WILLIAM SHAKESPEARE** was a popular playwright, poet and actor who lived in Elizabethan England. He married in Stratford-upon-Avon aged eighteen and had three children, although one died in childhood. Shakespeare then moved to London, where he wrote 39 plays and over 150 sonnets, many of which are still very popular today. In fact, his plays are performed more often than those of any other playwright, and he died 450 years ago! His gravestone includes a curse against interfering with his burial place, possibly to deter people from opening it in search of unpublished manuscripts. It reads, "Blessed be the man that spares these stones, and cursed be he that moves my bones." Spooky!

**MARCIA WILLIAMS'** mother was a novelist and her father a playwright, so it's not surprising that Marcia ended up an author herself. Although she never trained formally as an artist, she found that motherhood, and the time she spent later as a nursery school teacher, inspired her to start writing and illustrating children's books.

Marcia's books bring to life some of the world's all-time favourite stories and some colourful historical characters. Her hilarious retellings and clever observations will have children laughing out loud and coming back for more!

# More retellings from Marcia Williams

ISBN 978-1-4063-5692-2

ISBN 978-1-4063-5693-9

ISBN 978-1-4063-5694-6

ISBN 978-1-4063-5695-3

Available from all good booksellers

www.walker.co.uk